Overflowing for Santa

Willow Watkins

Copyright Page

Copyright 2025 by Willow Watkins

All rights reserved. No part of this publication may be reproduced, stored or transmitted in any form or by any means, electronic, mechanical, photocopying, recording, scanning or otherwise without written permission from the author. It is illegal to copy this book, post it to a website, or distribute it by any other means without permission.

This novel is entirely a work of fiction. The names, characters and incidents portrayed in it are the work of the authors imagination. Any resemblance to actual persons, living or dead, events or localities is entirely coincidental.

The characters depicted in this work of fiction are 18 years of age or older.

Contents

Chapter One	1
Chapter Two	7
Chapter Three	12
Chapter Four	18
Chapter Five	26
Chapter Six	33
Chapter Seven	39
Epilogue	48
About the Author	51

Chapter One

Nick

The velvet suit itches like hell. And the fake beard smells faintly of cinnamon and regret.

I shift in front of the full-length mirror, adjusting the thick belt across my waist for the fifth damned time. But no matter what I do, I still look like a bloated fool playing dress-up in a holiday commercial with all this padding around my middle.

Outside the dressing room door, I can hear them. Kids by the dozen, high on sugar and holiday adrenaline, their voices echoing through the vaulted wood-paneled hall of the community center. The kind of chaos that used to make my teeth grind. Still does, if I'm being honest.

I sigh, dragging a hand through my hair under the itchy white wig. *One day.* That's all I promised the PR team. One day playing Santa for the charity I've been funding anonymously for the last seven years. Usually I cut a big check, send a thank-you card, and get back to business. But apparently that's not "relatable" enough this year. Not for the man they're trying to rebrand as New York's Most Eligible Holiday Bachelor.

Ridiculous.

But the cause is solid. And if it means these kids get something to smile about, then I can swallow my pride for a few hours. Pose for some photos. Flash a jolly grin. Let them think Santa's real.

I'm grumbling under my breath when there's a knock on the door.

Before I can respond, it opens, and sunshine personified walks in wearing a Santa's helper costume. A short red velvet dress with white trim, striped tights, and curves that make the air in the room turn molten.

She's young. Early twenties, maybe. *Too young for me*, my brain says automatically. My body disagrees, violently.

Long, dark brown hair tumbles down her back in soft waves. Her skin's flushed, like she just came in from the snow, and those breasts that are barely restrained by the scooped neckline of her costume draw my eyes like gravity.

But it's her face that stops me completely.

Big blue eyes, shining like tinsel, framed by dark lashes. A wide, genuine smile that hits me like a sucker punch to the sternum.

I've met a thousand beautiful women. Dated models, socialites, actresses. But none of them have ever made me feel like I just forgot how to breathe.

She blinks up at me and beams. "Hi! You must be Mr. West. I'm Holly. I'm coordinating the Santa visit today."

Holly. Of course her name is Holly. Because she's the most Christmassy fucking thing I've ever seen, and I want to unwrap her on my lap and kiss every delicious-looking inch of her body.

I try to nod, but I think I'm growling.

"Oh," she says with a laugh, mistaking my silence for shyness. "Don't be nervous! You're gonna do great." Her voice is light and bubbly, full of excitement and warmth. "The kids have been lined up for over an hour, and they're super excited to meet Santa!"

Then, God help me, she reaches out and takes hold of my sleeve, her fingers curling into the thick red fabric as she tugs.

"Come on. They're waiting!"

I follow without hesitation. Not because of the PR team. Not for the cameras. But because she's the one leading me, and I'd follow that sway of her hips into actual hell.

My gaze drops to her back as she walks ahead, taking in the bounce of her ass and the way her striped tights stretch over those perfect curves. I want her bent over my desk. I want her on my lap. I want her under me with her legs locked around my waist while she milks me like the sweet little gift she is.

Fuck.

We emerge into the main hall. It's a wide open space strung with fairy lights and garlands, decked out in every shade of red and green imaginable. An ornate, oversized Santa chair sits at the center of the stage, already surrounded by bright-eyed children and exhausted parents.

I settle into the chair and plaster a smile on my face, raising a gloved hand in a wave.

But I don't see the crowd. Not really.

Because I can't take my eyes off Holly.

She moves with a graceful, light energy, like a sparkler flickering at the edge of my vision. One minute she's kneeling next to a toddler who won't let go of her candy cane, the next she's smoothing a little boy's hair before gently nudging him towards me.

"Go on, Santa doesn't bite," she says with a grin, and the boys light up as he approaches my chair.

I recover just in time to rumble out a hearty, "Ho, ho, ho! What's your name, little man?"

"Tyler," he whispers as I help him up onto my knee. His coat is too big for him, and his gloves don't match.

"Well, Tyler, I believe the elves told me you've been extra good this year..."

Holly's standing just behind him, beaming with pride like she's the one who raised him. And hell, the way she's leaning to talk to his mother with a hand on her arm, asking softly if they've got everything they need for the holidays, it does something to me.

There's a warm glow in my chest I haven't felt in a long time. Not since I made my first billion.

"Say thank you, Tyler," his mom calls as I hand him a gift wrapped in shiny red paper. The boy hugs it tight and hops down, beaming.

As they walk away, Holly guides in the next family with that same sunshine-drenched cheer. There's something different about her. She's not doing this because she has to. She wants to be here. She's not faking the warmth or the joy.

She's real.

And I can't stop staring.

The next family is a single mom with three kids under the age of six, all bundled up like marshmallows. One of the little girls tugs on the hem of Holly's skirt, asking if Santa's beard is real. Holly laughs and kneels to talk to her, explaining that Santa's beard grows magically longer every Christmas.

I'm supposed to be paying attention. I know that.

Instead, I'm watching Holly.

The way she smiles. The way the kids are drawn to her. The way her hand settles gently on the mother's shoulder, like she knows exactly how much weight that woman is carrying just to get through the damn day.

She'd be an amazing mother.

I don't even realize I'm gripping the arms of my chair until the wood creaks beneath my gloved hands. My thoughts spiral before I can stop them.

Not just a mother. *My* baby's mother.

Pregnant with my child. Glowing with it. Needy with it. Needing me. Letting me take care of her. Letting me worship her.

I shake myself. Jesus, pull it together. This is not the time or place.

And then she stands.

Holly rises from a crouch, brushing her hands down her skirt. She glances down at her front and stiffens, eyes going wide before she quickly crosses her arms over her chest.

But she wasn't quick enough. I saw it. The twin wet patches staining the front of her red dress right over her breasts, making the material turn dark. It's almost enough to make my brain short-circuit. She's lactating? Does she have children of her own? Well, her lack of a wedding ring, which had been one of the first things I checked out, means she's fair game as far as I'm concerned.

And she couldn't be any more perfect for me. The perfect mother of my future children.

She gives me a flustered, tight-lipped smile.

"I... uh... I just need to take a quick break," she says, already turning towards the side hall.

Another helper comes to take her place beside the queue. But I've already half-risen from my chair, my focus locked on Holly's retreating back.

She moves fast, practically disappearing into the staff hallway.

I want to follow her. Every cell in my body is screaming to go after her. To make sure she's okay. To find out what just happened. To touch her. Taste her.

But another child is nudged forward, and I lower myself slowly back into the chair.

I smile. Nod. Hand out another toy.

Meanwhile, my thoughts are dark and sharp and single-minded.

Holly's mine. And by the time I'm through with her, she'll never want anyone else. Ever.

Chapter Two

Holly

I've never been more grateful for an empty staff room.

I close the door behind me with a soft click and lean back against it, drawing in a long, shaky breath. My heart is still thudding in my chest, not from running around the event all morning, but from him.

The man in the red suit.

I grab my bag and sink down into one of the chairs, exhaling slowly and hoping it will calm the butterflies still going wild in my stomach. I should be focused on the event. On the kids we're helping and on the joy we're spreading.

But instead? I'm sitting here, cheeks burning, because I leaked in front of a billionaire of all people.

Great job, Holly.

I pull my pump out of the bag, put it all together, then pull my dress down and unclip one side of the nursing bra. When I place the pump over my nipple and press the button, it whirrs to life and suctions down. The feeling is weird and tingly, but it works, and a moment later, the first jet of liquid squirts out.

I breathe a sigh of relief as the pressure in my chest starts to ease.

It's not like I haven't had a few close calls since I started producing. I've always seemed to have an abundance of milk, and my body hasn't yet got the message that it's not needed anymore. But I've always managed to hide it, or rush off in time. Not today, though.

Not when he was watching me.

And Nick West was watching. I felt it. Every time I stepped close to him, it was like static clung to the air between us. His eyes never left me. And when I stood, glanced down, and saw the faint bloom of dampness across the red velvet of my costume, I didn't even have to look up to know he saw it too.

I cringe, and wish I could hide somewhere. "So much for keeping it a secret."

I try to remind myself that I'm being silly. That a man like him is rich, untouchable, and probably has a yacht named after some leggy blonde. He wouldn't give a second thought to some charity assistant with overactive mammary glands.

But I can't stop thinking about his eyes. The way they lingered.

A shiver runs down my spine, and for a single reckless heartbeat, I imagine what it would feel like if he came closer. If he reached for me. If his mouth was on my nipple instead of a pump right now, drawing the milk from my breast with an unquenchable thirst. Would he still look at me like that?

He's a billionaire. I'm the help. And I've got so much milk that he's bound to think I'm some kind of freak.

This is a disaster.

Besides, I don't even know what he looks like under that fake beard and long white wig. He could be a monster under there for all I know.

I sigh and switch off the pump, moving it to my other breast and repeating the process. I can hear the sound of kids squealing and laughing outside the door, but here, in this moment, it's quiet. Just me and the hum of the machine, and the feeling of the milk coming free, relieving the pressure.

I can't help the tiny, breathy moan that escapes. It feels good. Better than usual. Arousal flutters deep in my core.

And I know it's because of him. Because of the memory of his green eyes, sharp and possessive as they followed me around.

I close my eyes and try to push him from my mind, focusing on the task at hand. It takes a few more minutes, but soon, the milk is gone and my breasts feel comfortable again. I clip myself back into my bra, adjust my outfit, and put everything away, then reach into my bag to grab the Christmas sweater I brought with me in case something like this happened.

It's time to get back to work. And no matter what happens, or how appealing a certain Santa Claus is, I need to forget about him.

Because the truth is, men like him don't date women like me.

No matter how much I wish they would.

***

The room feels cavernous now that it's quiet. No more laughter. No more tiny footsteps pattering around the tree. No sticky fingers grabbing for candy canes or crinkling wrapping paper.

Just me and Santa... or rather, Nick, I guess.

Well, me, Nick, and a handful of staff from the charity milling around in the background quietly tidying up what's left of the event. But the only person I feel in the room is him. The air shifts when he's near, like gravity pulls harder. I hate how aware I am of him, even when I'm trying to focus on the empty tables where there had been stacks of gifts just a few hours ago.

Now there's nothing but tablecloths and glitter.

"I can't believe we ran out by lunchtime," I murmur under my breath, arms crossed tightly over my chest. "We shouldn't have opened the event to the public."

"What do you mean?" Nick's voice rumbles behind me, low and smooth now that he's not putting on the big, jolly act.

I sigh. "I told my boss it wasn't a good idea to open this up to the public. I mean, it always sounds great in theory. More reach means more families. But we didn't have enough for that many people. We just had enough for the families we already help year-round. And now..." I trail off, jaw tightening. "Now, a lot of them will go without. Again. It's bad enough that they have to do without so many things they need throughout the year because of their financial situation. The least they deserve is to have a special Christmas."

There's a long pause, then Nick asks, "Do you have a record of the families that usually receive help?"

I blink, surprised by the question. "Uh... yeah. We keep a database. Addresses, how many kids per household, ages. That sort of thing. Why?"

He doesn't answer immediately. I hear movement coming from behind me instead. The sound of fabric shifting.

When I turn to look at him, he's just taken off the Santa hat and beard, and for a second I forget how to breathe.

I... no. That cannot be what he actually looks like.

Strong jaw, perfectly carved cheekbones, five o'clock shadow dusting his sharp features. I knew he had the most gorgeous eyes I've ever seen, but I hadn't expected the rest of him to be so... perfect. He looks like a movie star who just walked off the set of a photo shoot.

My thoughts are still spinning when he starts stripping off the jacket, too. The red velvet drops away along with the padding he'd been wearing, and what's beneath it nearly knocks me off my feet. A tight white t-shirt hugs every inch of his broad chest and clings around his biceps. He's got the body of a man who's used to carrying the weight of the world... and tossing it aside when it doesn't serve him.

I stare. I shouldn't, but I can't help myself.

He notices, and one corner of his mouth curls up into a smirk.

"We're going shopping," he says finally. "I'm not letting a single name on that list go without something under the tree."

My mouth opens. Then closes. Then opens again. I think I nod. I'm not entirely sure my body is connected to my brain right now.

He steps closer. Not enough to touch me, but close enough that I can feel the heat coming off him. Close enough to smell his clean, masculine scent that's tinged with just a hint of cedar.

"Are you okay?" he asks softly. His eyes flicker briefly to my chest, but they are back on my face again so quickly that I'm not sure if I imagined it.

"I... yeah," I whisper, even though nothing about me feels okay in this moment. My chest feels tight. My skin tingles. My thoughts are like scrambled eggs in a frying pan. "It's just that you've already done so much. I don't want to..."

"You're not," he says, cutting me off with a voice that makes it clear he's made up his mind. "Let me just get changed and then we're going out. You'll pick out what you need for everybody, and I will pay for it."

He gives me one more lingering look and then turns and strides off towards the staff area to change out of the red pants.

And I'm left standing there, staring at the spot where he'd just been. Flushed. Breathless. Flustered.

And completely out of my depth.

Chapter Three

Nick

We're deep in the heart of the toy store, the scent of cinnamon and pine syrup clinging to the air, and I've got my hands wrapped around the handle of a cart piled high with gifts... but all I can really see is her.

Holly.

She's still wearing that little red dress with the white fur trim and the candy-cane striped tights, but now she's wearing a thick black jacket pulled over it. It does nothing to hide her curves, though. The layers hug her full chest, and those red-and-white tights wrap around legs that I'd like to feel wrapped around my neck sometime very soon.

She's a goddamn vision. A fever dream wrapped in red velvet.

And she smiles at me like I personally hung the damn stars in the sky.

"Thank you again," she says, cheeks flushed, eyes lit up like the top of the tree outside. "I still can't believe you're doing all this."

I grip the cart a little tighter. That smile of hers is dangerous. Lethal, even. It's enough to make me want to lose all control. "You don't have to thank me," I say, my voice coming out rougher than I mean it to. "I want to help. That's all."

And it's true. I've always wanted to help. That's why I've been sending checks to the charity for the last few years. But this year, it's different. I want to help her, too. Make her smile. Give her everything she wants and everything she never even dared to ask for.

There's literally nothing I wouldn't do to make my woman beam with happiness like she has been during this entire shopping trip. And she hasn't even asked for anything for herself. All she wants is to help the families who can't afford to help themselves right now, and I'm here to make it happen any way I can.

We both push our overflowing carts towards the counter where four more carts are already waiting to be paid for. One of the store clerks lets out a low whistle.

"Ring them all up," I tell him. "We'll be back in a few."

Holly laughs softly beside me as we step away. "I think they're scared you're going to buy the entire store."

"I might," I murmur, offering her a sidelong look. "Depends how much more you smile at me like that."

She blinks, caught off guard, and the heat that rushes to her cheeks almost makes me groan. She's so sweet. So soft and earnest. She doesn't even realize what she's doing to me.

Or realize how much I'm going to enjoy ruining her once I get her alone.

We leave the store behind and make our way towards a small kiosk selling hot drinks. After asking her what she wants, I buy us both a hot chocolate with the works - marshmallows and whipped cream. I hand Holly her cup, and with one hand on the small of her back, I lead her towards the giant Christmas tree in the center of the mall.

It towers overhead. Carolers are singing somewhere in the distance. A couple is taking a photo with their toddler near the tree's base.

And Holly... she just stares up at it like she's never seen anything so magical.

I stare at her the same way.

I want her. Hell. I want to keep her forever.

We both stand in silence for a moment while we take sips from our mugs, letting the warmth of the drink seep into our bodies. I should say something. I should focus on the shopping still ahead. But instead, what comes out is:

"Do you have any little ones at home to shop for?"

She turns to me, blinking. "What?"

"You know," I say, careful to keep my tone light, "a baby, maybe. Someone you're buying gifts for."

The question has been burning me up inside ever since I first saw those two dark patches on the front of her dress. I couldn't hold it back anymore. I need to know if she already belongs to someone else.

"Oh... no," she says quickly, cheeks burning a deeper shade of pink. "No babies of my own."

She laughs nervously, and it's adorable. But I press gently. "I thought maybe you did. You know, since..."

Since I saw her leaking. Since my brain short-circuited with a thousand different thoughts, most of them involving sucking one of her nipples deep into my mouth and tasting her sweet milk for the very first time.

She clears her throat, clearly flustered. "Oh. No. That's actually... a long story. My sister had twins last year. Two beautiful girls. But she had a rough delivery, and her milk never really came in. I offered to help, and I induced lactation so my sister could feed them my milk. Just until they got bigger and healthier and could switch to formula."

My chest tightens. The thought of her doing something so selfless makes my fists clench. It's not just that she's got milk... though that alone is already enough to drive me to the edge of my sanity. It's what it means. Her instinct is to nurture. Her willingness to give her body over to care for someone else's babies.

She was made to be a mother, and I already know my children would never want for anything if they had her.

I have no doubt that when she's big and round with my baby growing inside her, she'll be glowing and even more beautiful than she is now.

She clears her throat again, pulling me out of my possessive thoughts. "Sorry, that was probably more than you wanted to know."

"No," I say, voice low. "It wasn't."

She looks up at me then, searching, and I take that moment to ask the question that's playing on my mind. "Do you want kids someday?"

She blushes again but doesn't look away. "Yeah. More than anything. But I'm twenty-two and... and I've never even really had a boyfriend. Apparently, it's difficult to find a man who is okay with... with all this." She gestures vaguely to her chest.

And just like that, I know.

I'm not just going to fuck her. I'm going to claim her. Breed her.

Keep her full and swollen for the rest of her life.

I lean down, brushing my lips against her ear. "Well, now you've found a man who is much more than okay with everything about you, princess. A man who can't wait to give you all the babies you could ever desire."

She lets out a soft gasp and pulls back just enough to look up into my eyes. But my gaze is drawn down to her mouth, to the soft pink lips that are parted in surprise. My heart is racing, and my dick is hard as a rock inside my pants, straining painfully against the material.

Before I can close the distance between us, she takes a step back, her face flushed. But even through the layers she's wearing, I can see the rapid rise and fall of her chest.

She turns the conversation then, tugging me back from the edge of a very filthy mental spiral. "I know you've always donated to this charity, and it's incredibly generous of you. But why this one in particular?"

I hesitate, but only for a beat. She deserves the truth.

"I grew up in a family with no money," I say. "My mom raised four of us after my dad died. There were years we didn't have a Christmas tree. Barely had heat. If a charity like this had existed back then..." I shrug. "I guess I just want to help kids growing up in the same kind of situation I did."

She stares at me for a long moment. "That's... incredible, Nick. Or maybe I should call you Saint Nick?"

Her lips quirk up into a grin, and I can't help but laugh. "I'm not even close to being a saint, Holly. I can promise you that."

"I don't know," she says softly. "You might be closer than you think."

This time, she's the one to lean in, and she presses a kiss to my cheek. Soft. Warm. Reverent.

When she doesn't pull back right away, I tilt my head. My lips brush hers. Featherlight. But the sound she makes - soft, breathy, needy - makes my control snap taut.

I step back before I do something reckless. Like drag her into the nearest storage closet, rip her clothes off, and fill her with my seed while I drain her full tits.

Yeah, I'm a long way from being a fucking saint.

"We should get back to shopping," I say, voice thick with restraint.

She blinks, dazed. "We've already got all the toys."

I grab her hand, feeling how small and soft it is in mine, and tug her forward. "We're getting some essentials too. Hats. Gloves. Scarves. Pajamas. Blankets. And then we are going back to my place to put them all together into packages for each family."

She starts to protest again, but I cut her off with a look. One that says I'm not taking no for an answer.

She follows, breathless and pink-cheeked, and my dick is harder than the concrete beneath our feet.

Holding onto my self-control today is going to be a sweet fucking torture.

But it's a torture I'll gladly suffer for her.

Anything for my girl.

Chapter Four

Holly

The elevator doors slide open, and I step into Nick's penthouse like I'm stepping into another world.

Marble floors gleam beneath my feet. Soft lighting glows from chandeliers that probably cost more than the amount still left to pay on my student loans. Everything smells faintly of cedarwood and clean linen, and the windows stretch from floor to ceiling, giving a glittering view of the city skyline wrapped in a blanket of December snow. There's a real fireplace crackling in one corner, the flames dancing like something out of a holiday movie. It's beautiful. Warm. Quiet.

And completely surreal.

I've never been in a place like this before. It feels like walking into the pages of a luxury lifestyle magazine... one where I definitely don't belong. My coat feels cheaper here. My boots more scuffed. The soft velvet dress suddenly feels juvenile in comparison to all this masculine sophistication.

Nick, on the other hand, fits here like he was born in this kind of power, even though I know the truth about his childhood now. He's calm. Confident. His expensive wool coat is draped over one of the armchairs, and the sleeves of his sweater are rolled up as he oversees the deliveries like a general commanding troops.

"Set those by the far wall. Be careful with the boxes marked fragile." His voice is low and assured, and every time he speaks, people move.

While we were driving back, the courier service he'd hired were way ahead of us, transporting all our shopping to his place. Building staff helped run the packages up to the penthouse via the private elevator. And now it looks like Santa's warehouse exploded across his living room, with bags and boxes stuffed with toys and all other kinds of supplies strewn everywhere.

It's chaos. Organized chaos, but still chaos. And all of it... for the kids.

I bite my lip as I watch Nick slip folded bills into each staff member's palm and thank them with a firm shake of the hand and a rare smile. The men leave beaming as they check out their generous tips.

And then it's just us.

Silence settles over the room like snow. I'm standing there in my candy-cane tights, charity-issue festive dress, and a Christmas sweater to hide the stains left there earlier by my little accident. I feel very much like the girl who doesn't belong at the ball, but then I glance up and...

Nick is staring at me.

There's a look in his eyes that could melt every inch of snow in the city. Dark. Hungry. Possessive.

I'm suddenly all too aware of the feeling in my chest. Full. Heavy. Like one look from him is enough to have me ready to burst. God, if I start leaking in front of him again today, it will just be even more humiliating.

"Ummm, before we get started on putting together all these packages, I should probably... well, I need to pump."

My face is burning, and I have no doubt that I must be bright red right now. Even though he didn't show any outward disgust when we talked about it by the Christmas tree at the mall, it's still not the kind of thing that normal people talk about with someone they've only known for a few hours.

I look away and reach for my bag on the couch. But before I can touch it, Nick is in front of me, his large hand wrapped gently around my wrist.

"No, Holly," he says, his voice deep and rough. "You don't need the pump anymore. Not now you've got me."

Got him? I don't need the pump? His closeness is affecting my ability to think straight, and it's not until he's tugging my sweater off over my head that I realize what he means.

"Nick, what..."

His eyes darken. "Let me take care of you, princess."

His voice is thick with a kind of restrained need. The kind that makes every muscle in my body turn to jelly.

And when his big, strong hands close over my breasts, kneading the swollen flesh gently through the material of my dress, I can't even find the strength to argue. Why would I want to? Isn't this the exact moment I've been hoping for ever since I first saw him earlier today?

I reach back and lower the zipper of my dress, and before my hands are even at my sides again, Nick's already sliding the soft material off my shoulders and down my arms. He peels the fabric from my body and lets it fall to the ground, leaving me in only my bra, panties, and the candy-cane tights.

He's staring down at me like a king surveying his kingdom, and the fire burning in his eyes is almost enough to set me alight.

I stand there, exposed and trembling, nipples already straining against the thin fabric of my bra, and wait for him to say something.

But instead, he reaches around and unclasps the bra, tugging the straps free from my arms and tossing the garment aside.

His hands slide over the soft, full flesh of my chest. They are so warm. So large. I can feel the calluses on his fingers from a lifetime of hard work.

"You're perfect," he murmurs, thumbs stroking over the tight buds of my nipples. "Perfect for me."

Suddenly, he takes a step back, pulling his hand away from my breast, and I can't stop the needy whimper that escapes me at the loss of his touch. But he takes a seat on the couch before grabbing my hand and tugging me onto his lap.

I'm straddling his thighs, and it's impossible to ignore the way his erection presses against my core.

"You have no idea how much I've wanted you," he whispers, hands sliding up my sides, his touch leaving goosebumps in its wake. "How much I've wanted to taste you. It's all I've been able to think about all fucking day. Ever since I saw those wet patches on your dress..."

I let out a gasp as he ducks his head, pressing his face into the valley between my breasts. The groan that escapes him is almost animalistic. My heart is hammering against my rib cage. My hands are clutching his broad shoulders.

And when his mouth closes over one nipple, drawing it deep, a jolt of pure pleasure shoots down to my clit.

"Oh my god."

Pressure builds up inside me for one dizzying moment before I feel that first rush of milk spurting into his mouth. He grunts, the sound vibrating through my entire body, and I can feel his hands gripping my ass cheeks as he holds me tightly against him.

The sensation is... intense. So much more than when I use the pump. It's a hot rush of relief, and a throb of desire, and a need so raw and aching that it makes my head spin.

I grind against him, shamelessly rubbing my soaked panties against his cock, and he just holds me tighter. Devouring me. Consuming me. Drinking from me like I'm the only source of sustenance in his world.

When he pulls away from my nipple, it's with a loud pop, and the look in his eyes is enough to send me reeling. His pupils are blown wide. His mouth and chin are dripping wet. He licks his lips, tongue sliding across his mouth and cleaning the milk off his skin.

"Holly," he growls.

Then his lips crash into mine, and I taste myself on him. My sweetness. The rich, creamy flavor of my own milk.

I kiss him back, clinging to him like he's the only solid thing in the world. And maybe he is. My entire existence seems to have shrunk down to this moment, this man, this connection.

My hands slide up into his hair, and his tongue dips between my lips, exploring my mouth like he can't get enough. My nipples rub against his sweater, and the soft material makes them ache, making more milk leak from the tight buds.

Nick is the first to break away, his breathing heavy. His expression is dark and dangerous. His eyes are locked on my mouth, and I can see the hunger written in every line of his face.

"Whenever you're full and need relief from now on, you'll come to me. Is that understood? Your milk is mine, and I want every fucking drop."

His voice is a deep growl that sends a shiver down my spine.

I nod quickly, feeling flushed and needy and breathless.

He gives a sharp nod, as if he's satisfied with my response. Then his mouth moves to my other nipple, and his lips close over it, drawing the tight bud deep.

"Oh God," I whisper, fingers curling into the material of his sweater. "Yes."

This time, I feel his teeth graze the sensitive flesh, and the bolt of pure lust that shoots through me almost knocks the breath from my lungs. It's too much. It's not enough.

It's everything.

Nick's arms are wrapped around me, holding me tightly against him, and he drinks from me while I writhe in his lap. My panties are soaked through, and every shift and flex of my hips has my throbbing clit brushing against the thick ridge of his cock.

I've never felt this desperate for release. This wild and out of control.

"Please," I beg, breathless. "I need... oh God..."

Nick grunts, his teeth digging into the soft flesh around my nipple. And then his hand is sliding between us, pressing against my mound through the tights and panties. His finger finds my clit, circling and stroking the swollen bud through the material.

I'm so worked up that I come apart faster than I ever imagined possible, crying out as wave after wave of pleasure crashes over me. Nick holds me tightly, his mouth still latched onto my breast, his hand rubbing between my thighs, drawing out the climax until it leaves me shaking and weak and utterly spent.

When I finally come back to myself, Nick has released my nipple and is lapping gently at the wet, tender flesh, soothing away the ache with his tongue. He looks up, meeting my gaze, and the fire that burns in his eyes almost sets me alight.

"Good girl," he says softly. "You look so beautiful when you come for me, princess. But next time, I'll be buried inside you when you fall apart. You're mine, Holly. And I'm going to breed you until you're nice and full and round with my baby. I can't wait to watch your belly grow big and heavy while your tits swell even bigger, ready to nurture our child."

His words send a fresh rush of desire through me, and I can't help but whimper at the thought. The idea of having a baby with him, of being his, fills me with a fierce longing.

"You want that, don't you?" he asks, his voice low and rough.

"Yes," I whisper, nodding eagerly. "Yes, please. I want everything."

He growls and tilts his head, pressing his forehead against mine. "First, we are going to prepare all these packages, and get them delivered. Then I'm going to fuck you and fill you with my seed, and make you come over and over and over. You'll be so full of my cum, there won't be a single doubt in your mind that I've claimed you. You'll belong to me, princess. Always."

A shiver of anticipation runs down my spine at the thought. "Do we really have to wait?" I ask in a breathless voice, not caring how shameless I might sound.

"Fuck, Holly. I love knowing how eager you are for me to claim you," he growls, shifting his hips to press his erection against my core. "But I know that once I sink my dick into your hot, wet cunt, I won't ever want to stop. So we are going to get these gift parcels prepared and delivered, and then I'm going to take you to my bed and fuck you until the only word you can remember is my name."

I let out a whimper at his words, and the feeling of his thick cock pressed against me. My entire body is buzzing with desire, and I can feel the tension coiled tightly in every muscle.

"Okay," I say, reluctantly easing off his lap. "If we're going to do this, we'd better get started."

He grins up at me, the hunger in his gaze taking my breath away. "That's my girl."

Chapter Five

Nick

We've been at this all night.

The sun hasn't even thought about rising yet, and still... we work.

The floor of my penthouse is a sea of ribbons and gift wrap, boxes and tissue paper. There's Christmas music humming low from the speakers. We're surrounded by hundreds of packages, each one carefully filled with toys, scarves, hats, socks, and other essentials we picked out together hours ago. And somehow, even though we're running on fumes, I feel wired. Awake. Alive in a way I haven't felt in years.

Because she's here.

My girl. My Holly.

She's sitting cross-legged beside me on the floor, curls falling loose around her flushed cheeks, a roll of red ribbon tucked between her knees as she carefully ties a bow. She's still in that little red dress, teasing me with the sight of those dried milk stains on the front, reminding me how goddamn perfect she'd tasted.

I'm so fucking thirsty for more, but I can't get distracted. Not when we've got work to do.

And she's enough of a distraction as it is. All she has to do is exist, and it's enough to have my entire universe spinning around her.

Every time her soft shoulder brushes against mine, I have to stop myself from pulling her into my lap. Every time she leans forward and her sweet, warm scent drifts to me, my cock twitches, hard and insistent inside my pants.

All I can think about is her skin against mine. Her mouth. Her milk. Her thighs wrapped around my hips as I fill her so deep she forgets about every other man in the world. I know she said she hasn't really had a boyfriend, but I've got no idea if she's ever hooked up with anyone else.

God, please let me be the only one who gets to claim her.

Holly stifles a yawn and glances at the final pile of supplies still waiting to be bundled. "Think we can finish this last one before I pass out on your living room floor?"

I grin and then lean down to kiss the top of her head, brushing my lips gently against silky brown waves.

"Let's do it together."

And we do.

When the last ribbon is tied, and the last label affixed, I sit back with a quiet exhale. Holly stretches her arms over her head and lets out a groan so sinfully sweet I have to clench my jaw to stop myself from grabbing her and bending her over the nearest surface.

Instead, I stand and gather her up in my arms.

She lets out a sleepy giggle, her cheek resting against my chest. "Nick..."

"Hush," I murmur, nuzzling my face in her hair. "You've worked hard. We both have."

"But the delivery..."

"Doesn't happen for a few more hours," I remind her. "You're taking a nap. I'm not letting you burn out before we get those packages where they need to go."

She doesn't argue.

Not when I carry her into the bedroom. Not when I lay her down on cool, crisp sheets and pull the duvet up to her chin.

Not even when I climb in beside her, wrapping my arms around her and pulling her close until her back is pressed to my chest and her round ass is nestled perfectly against me.

She shifts slightly to get comfortable, and her butt rubs against my dick.

Fuck.

It's a sweet torture. One that has my cock painfully hard and throbbing with need.

Holly is warm and soft and fucking perfect. The weight of her in my arms is the most wonderful kind of torment. And if I have my way, this is how I will be falling asleep every night for the rest of my life, with the woman of my dreams in my arms like this.

I wait for her breathing to even out, but it doesn't. It stays shallow and rapid, her heart pounding against my forearm, her hips rolling ever so slightly against me.

"Sleep, Holly," I murmur, lips brushing against the soft skin at the base of her neck.

"Can't."

"And why's that, princess?"

She hesitates a beat before answering. "Because... I want to give you some relief too, Nick. You're so hard, and I don't like knowing you're suffering because of me."

Fuck.

"I already told you I plan to wait before taking you, so I can keep you moaning for hours, princess," I say firmly, surprising myself with how gruff my voice sounds. "Once all the gifts are delivered, then I'll make sure you know exactly who you belong to."

Holly turns in my arms to face me, placing a hand on my chest before slowly trailing it lower. I hold my breath, my cock so fucking hard now that it feels like it's trying to tunnel its way through my pants.

"I understand that," she says, "but there are other things I could do to help you feel a little better, right?"

I open my mouth to answer, but at that moment, her hand moves even lower to cup my aching cock through the fabric, and every rational thought I had vanishes.

"Please," she says, her voice a low whisper.

I know I should let her sleep now. It's almost four in the morning. We've had a long day, and we've got another one ahead of us. But the selfish desire to have my girl take care of the ache in my groin is too strong to resist.

"You want to put that pretty mouth on my cock, princess?" I ask, the words coming out low and husky.

"Yes." Her answer is immediate, her cheeks flushing a deeper pink.

I can't believe this woman. Every time I think she can't be any more perfect, she proves me wrong.

"Then go ahead. Show me how much you want to help."

Her eyes are wide and hungry as she pulls the covers back and reaches for the zipper of my pants. A groan escapes my throat when she slides her hand beneath the fabric and wraps it around the base of my shaft, her fingers barely able to touch.

"Fuck, Holly," I grit out, reaching down to help her free my cock.

I can't remember the last time I was this hard. The last time someone had touched me with such care and reverence. I know I should slow her down, take it easy and savor every moment, but fuck, it's so goddamn good.

The feeling of her soft hand stroking the length of my shaft. The way her eyes light up when a drop of precum beads at the tip. The sound of her ragged breathing.

It's enough to drive a man crazy.

"God, you're big," she breathes, her voice full of awe. "I don't know if I can take all of you. This is my first time."

"Don't worry, princess. Just do what feels natural. If it gets too much, just use your hands and mouth," I tell her.

She nods and ducks her head, pressing her lips to the tip in a sweet kiss. Then she opens her mouth and takes the head inside.

Holy. Fuck.

My whole body tenses at the feeling of her warm, wet mouth enveloping the head of my dick. It's all I can do to stop myself from gripping her hair and thrusting into her throat.

"That's it, princess," I encourage her, stroking her hair. "Good girl."

I keep my eyes locked on her as she begins to bob her head up and down, taking more of my length with each stroke. She looks so beautiful, kneeling beside me, sucking my cock. Her lips are stretched wide around my girth, her cheeks flushed pink, and her eyes are full of heat and desire.

"Fuck, you're a fast learner," I grunt, fisting her hair gently. "That's my girl. Such a good cocksucker."

She whimpers, the vibration sending shivers through my body, and I can't help but push a little further into her mouth. She takes it without complaint, and when her tongue slides along the underside of my shaft, I groan and tighten my grip on her hair.

"Such a good fucking girl," I praise her, my voice thick with lust. "Your mouth feels so fucking good."

I can feel the pressure building at the base of my spine. Every lick, every suck, is taking me closer and closer to the edge. And when she moans again, the vibrations traveling along my cock and making my balls tighten, I know I won't be able to hold back much longer.

"Holly, fuck, princess, I'm gonna come," I growl. "You want to taste my cum, Holly? You want to swallow every drop?"

She doesn't hesitate. She just sucks harder, her hand working the base of my shaft in tandem.

I'm lost.

I'm fucking done.

With a low grunt, I explode into her mouth, my cock pulsing as thick ropes of cum paint her tongue. She swallows greedily, taking everything I have to give, and the look of pure ecstasy on her face as she does sends another shudder of pleasure through me.

When I'm finally spent, I slump back against the pillows, panting for air. Holly releases my cock and sits back on her heels, a soft smile playing on her lips.

"Was that okay?" she asks, her voice shy and a little hesitant.

"More than okay," I say, reaching out to pull her into my arms. "It was perfect."

She snuggles into me, resting her head on my chest. "Good."

We lay like that for a while, our breathing slowly returning to normal. My eyelids grow heavy, and I'm just about to drift off when Holly speaks again, her voice soft and sleepy.

"Nick?"

"Mm?"

"Thank you. For everything."

I smile, the darkness closing in. "You're welcome, princess."

As I drift off, my mind is filled with thoughts of Holly. Her warmth. Her softness. The taste of her milk. The feel of her mouth around my cock.

And as my body relaxes, the scent of her fills my nose. The warmth of her breath tickles the skin on my neck.

This is where she belongs. In my arms. Where she will stay forever.

Chapter Six

Holly

I can't stop smiling.

The truck rumbles beneath us as we turn another corner, the festive bells strung across the windscreen jingling softly with every bump in the road. Warm air blows from the vents, fogging up the windows slightly, and everything is a blur of gray slush and snow-covered rooftops. But inside the cab, it's like a little pocket of holiday magic.

Nick rented this truck just for today, Christmas Eve, and even went as far as paying someone at the rental place a ridiculous tip to decorate it overnight for us. There's a garland framing the dashboard, a tiny fiber-optic tree blinking merrily in the cupholder, and Christmas music plays cheerfully from the speakers mounted on the roof of the truck, drifting out into the frosty morning air for everyone to hear. It should be cheesy. Over the top.

But somehow, when it's him, it just makes my chest feel full and fuzzy and warm.

He glances over at me, all dressed up in that Santa suit again. The beard is full and fluffy, his cheeks dusted with just enough blush to look like he's stepped in from the North Pole. The hat sits slightly askew over snow-white curls, and his red coat stretches comfortably over the convincing belly padding beneath. With his gloved hands on the wheel and that twinkle in his eye, he looks every bit the picture-perfect Santa Claus.

And beside him? Me.

Mrs. Claus.

Or at least... my best attempt. A clean new dress that fits like a dream. Nipped at the waist, soft red velvet with snow-white faux fur at the collar and hem. He bought it for me yesterday at the mall, along with the matching red cloak and little red gloves. I'd protested at the time, cheeks burning, but he just murmured *"Santa takes care of his wife"* and pressed the bag into my hands.

And just like that... I was ruined for anyone else.

Forever.

And he has taken good care of me since we met. Even this morning, when I'd woken with my breasts feeling sore and full, he'd taken his time nursing from me, sucking gently at the tender flesh until my nipples were swollen and aching. And when he'd slipped a finger into the slick folds between my thighs, it was like heaven.

His touch has been electric. His kisses, magical.

I already know that my first time with him is going to be mind-blowing, and I can't wait for it. But for now, we have more important things to focus on.

"Ready?" he rumbles as we pull up in front of the first house.

I nod, nerves and excitement fluttering in my belly. "Let's do this."

We climb down from the truck and make our way up the walkway, arms full of carefully bundled gifts and essentials. The sun is barely up, but already, someone's peeking through the curtains.

A moment later, the front door swings open, and a woman with tired eyes and a toddler balanced on her hip gasps in shock.

"Santa?" she breathes, blinking at us like we're an illusion. "Oh my God, it's really…"

"Merry Christmas!" Nick booms, slipping seamlessly into character. His voice is deep and jolly, his laugh warm and rich as he gestures to the gifts in our arms. "We heard you've been very good this year."

The toddler stares at him with wide eyes, then hides his face in his mother's neck.

Another child, a little girl of maybe six or seven, comes racing down the hall, squealing with delight when she sees the man in red.

"Santa! Mommy, it's really Santa!"

My throat tightens as I kneel to pass her a brightly wrapped package. Her eyes sparkle with pure joy as she clutches it to her chest like it's the most precious thing in the world.

Beside me, Nick holds out a soft pink teddy bear to the toddler, who is now reaching out curiously. "This is for you, little one."

The mother has tears in her eyes now. Quiet, overwhelmed as she takes the rest of the bags from my arms.

"I don't know what to say," she whispers. "This is… this is everything. I don't know how to thank you."

Nick reaches out and gently touches her shoulder. "You don't need to thank us. Just take care of your beautiful babies. That's all the thanks we need."

The woman nods, and I swear, if I wasn't already in love with this man, that would have done it.

We say our goodbyes, and as we walk back to the truck, I glance sideways at him.

He's grinning beneath the beard, and his hand brushes the small of my back in a way that makes my pulse stutter.

"How'd I do?" he murmurs under his breath.

I smile so wide it almost hurts.

"Perfect," I whisper.

***

The day passes in a blur of magic and warmth.

Family after family, smile after smile.

Some cry. Some laugh. Some don't know what to say at all. But every single one of them lights up when they see him. Santa, bringing joy and relief to families that needed both so badly. And beside him, I play my role. Smiling, hugging, handing out packages, offering warm words to tired parents and squealing children.

And all the while, my heart is swelling with something dangerous.

Because I know it's crazy. I know I've only known him a single day. But I've never met a man like Nick. Never imagined someone so generous and so gentle. All the stories I've heard in the media about the greed and selfishness of billionaires had made me think Nick would be the same. But he's not. He's so... quietly good. Ever since the photographers left the event yesterday, he hasn't taken a single picture or spoken to a single person about what he's doing. This isn't a PR stunt. This is... just who he is.

And the way he is with these kids is making me ache.

Because all I can think about is what he'd be like with our children.

Strong and kind. Steady. Protective. A man who would make any sacrifice to give his babies everything they need.

And God help me... I want it.

I want all of it.

***

The sun has started to dip low in the sky, casting golden streaks across the snow-covered rooftops as we pull up to the last house on our list. My feet ache, my curls are frizzing out of my hood, and I'm pretty sure my cheeks are permanently rosy from the cold and smiling so much. But I've never felt more full. My heart, not my chest, though... that too.

Apparently, just being around Nick, and knowing how much he enjoys feeding from me, is enough to send my milk production into overdrive.

He hops down from the truck first, still booming out his deep, jovial *"Ho ho ho!"* as he gathers the final gift bags. The Christmas music playing from the rooftop speakers rolls out softly around us like a festive lullaby for the neighborhood. I grab the last few parcels and follow him up the little garden path to the front door, where two wide-eyed siblings peek out through the frosted window, bouncing with excitement.

Their mother opens the door with a tired but grateful smile, and her hand flies to her mouth as she takes in the mountain of gifts we're carrying.

"Santa...?" the little boy whispers, his voice full of awe.

Nick crouches down, grinning behind his beard. "That's me, buddy. I heard you and your sister have been very good this year."

The little girl squeals, and I kneel to open one of the bags, pulling out a doll dressed in a glittery red gown. Her gasp is pure wonder.

"Is this... really for me?" she breathes.

"All yours," I tell her with a wink. "And there's more inside. But you'll have to wait until tomorrow morning to open those."

The mother blinks fast, trying to hold back tears as she takes the parcels from me. "I don't know what to say. Thank you so much."

Nick rests a gloved hand on her shoulder. "Just promise me you'll have a beautiful Christmas together. That's all I need."

We leave them waving and calling out *"Merry Christmas!"* behind us, and as we climb back into the truck, my heart swells to the point I think it might burst.

Nick slides into the driver's seat, turning towards me slowly. The Santa beard has shifted a little, revealing just a hint of chiseled jaw beneath, and his voice drops low.

"That's the last stop, Mrs. Claus," he murmurs. "Now it's time for me to take you home."

I blink up at him, dazed from emotion and the way he's looking at me like I'm the only thing in his world.

He leans in slightly, eyes hot behind all the fluff and velvet. "It's time for me to give you a special gift."

My breath catches.

He brushes a hand over my stomach and murmurs. "A baby. Right here. In this sweet little belly."

My thighs clench. My lips part.

And just like that, the sleigh ride is over. Because my body is already desperate for what comes next.

He starts the engine, and as we pull away from the curb, the only thing louder than the Christmas music outside... is the pounding of my heart inside.

Chapter Seven

Nick

The penthouse is dark when we step inside, the city twinkling far below us through the floor-to-ceiling windows. Holly follows me in, hugging her arms around herself, her breath misting the air in a soft little puff.

I head straight for the fireplace.

The electric kind would've been easier, sure. But I've always preferred the real thing. There's something primal about it. The snap and hiss of wood catching flame. The way heat licks through the chill and wraps itself around you like a living thing.

I crouch down and strike the match, focusing on the task even as I feel her behind me.

The fire catches fast. It always does when I build it. I've got a rhythm to it, a system. Kindling tucked beneath the perfectly cut logs. Airflow just right. One spark, and the whole thing roars to life, golden and alive.

Like me.

Because every second she's standing behind me, I can feel the tension building. Can hear the silence thickening. The air between us is practically humming. The kind of charged stillness that comes right before something irreversible happens.

I rise slowly and take a step back away from the fireplace, not turning around right away. I take my time, peeling off the thick red coat and tugging away the padding beneath it, letting it fall with a quiet thud to the floor. Next goes the beard, the hat, the ridiculous wig.

Then I turn, and there she is.

Standing in front of the Christmas tree, bathed in warm light from the fire and fairy lights alike. Her Mrs. Claus dress clings to her curves, her curls falling over her shoulders like something out of a dream. Her lips are parted. Her breath shallow.

She doesn't say a word.

Neither do I.

I just drink her in for a long moment, savoring every inch of her. And when her eyes finally meet mine, wide and wonderstruck... I know she's ready for this.

Ready for me.

I take a step closer to her, hearing the way her breath catches as I reach for the hem of my shirt and pull it up and off. My hands move to the buttons of my pants, and she watches, transfixed, as I free myself and kick away the rest.

In moments, I'm completely bare. Hard and pulsing. Ready for her.

I move slowly, giving her a chance to back away, but she doesn't. She's trembling slightly, but not with fear. Her eyes are locked on my cock, and her hands are moving slowly, fingers curling and uncurling like she wants to touch me but isn't quite brave enough.

I stop in front of her and take her chin between my fingers, tilting her face up.

"Are you scared, princess?"

She shakes her head.

"No? Not even a little bit?"

She bites her lip and murmurs, "Not of you."

It's so soft, I can barely hear it. But it's enough to make my heart stutter.

I brush a finger along her cheek, tracing her jawline, watching the way her pupils dilate and her cheeks flush.

"There's no reason to be," I murmur, cupping her face in my hand. "Not with me."

"I know," she breathes.

Her eyes drift down again, and her hand lifts to my stomach, just the barest whisper of fingertips grazing the muscles. It takes all my willpower not to rip her dress off and drag her down to the floor so I can bury myself inside her.

But she's new to this. New to everything. And I'll be damned if I let her first time be anything less than perfect.

Holly takes another step closer, until there is barely any space between our bodies, and she leans in to brush her lips against my chest, over the spot where my heart races.

"Holly..."

She kisses my skin again, and then her teeth catch the edge of my collarbone. My hands find her hips, and I squeeze, drawing a little whimper from her lips.

"God, princess," I groan, my cock jerking against her stomach. "You're killing me."

She doesn't respond, just presses another kiss to the column of my throat. Her fingers curl against my chest, her nails scraping gently against my bare skin, and I can feel the desperation rolling off her in waves.

My control is slipping, and fast.

I need her.

Need her so fucking badly.

"Do you have any idea what you're doing to me?" I growl, fisting a hand in her hair and tugging gently.

Her breath hitches, and her eyelashes flutter as she looks up at me.

"Yes," she whispers. "The same thing you're doing to me."

The thin thread of restraint snaps.

I crush my lips to hers, and the taste of her sends my senses into overdrive. Her hands are on my shoulders, clinging to me, and I can feel the heat of her through the layers of velvet between us. I'm burning up, consumed by the need to claim her, and her small gasps only stoke the flames.

My hands are on her dress, yanking the fabric up and over her head. It pools on the floor, and her hair cascades down her bare shoulders. My palms find the warm skin of her back, and I pull her close, my mouth devouring hers.

Her breasts are full and heavy, and when I nudge my thigh between hers, I can feel the wetness between her legs soaking through the panties. My cock throbs, aching to be inside her, but I resist the urge. I want to taste her first. Want to make her come with my tongue, my fingers, before I fill her with my seed and fuck a baby into her.

"Nick..." she whimpers, and the sound of her voice is almost enough to break me.

"I've got you," I growl, lifting her and laying her down gently on the rug in front of the fire.

She looks up at me, her cheeks flushed, her eyes bright, and I can't believe she's mine. That this incredible woman chose me, even for a moment.

I kneel between her legs, and my hands trail down her body, lingering on the curves of her hips, the swell of her breasts. I trace the line of her panties, and she arches up, seeking my touch.

"Please..."

I tug the fabric down her legs, and she's finally bared to me. Vulnerable. Soft and aching.

She's perfect.

"So fucking beautiful," I murmur, pressing a kiss to her inner thigh.

My lips trail upwards, and her fingers tangle in my hair, her hips shifting restlessly beneath me.

When I reach the top of her thigh, I can smell her arousal. She's dripping for me, and the scent is intoxicating. I lean in and lick a slow line up the center of her folds, and her moan is the sweetest thing I've ever heard.

"Oh my God," she gasps, and I smile against her.

"Just wait, princess."

I tease her clit with my tongue, drawing tight circles around the swollen bud, and her body shudders. Her hands are still tangled in my hair, and she's pulling hard now, her breath coming in short, sharp gasps.

I dip a finger into her entrance, and the heat and tightness of her is enough to make my cock leak. She's so wet, so ready for me, and I can't wait to sink into her. But first, I want to make her come.

I push another finger inside her, curling them just right, and she lets out a broken moan.

"Nick, I..."

Her words dissolve into a cry as I suck her clit, and her body shudders. She's close, so close, and I can feel the walls of her pussy fluttering around my fingers.

I press a third finger into her, preparing her for my girth, and she arches off the floor, her thighs clamping around my head.

"Come for me," I growl. "Come on my face, princess. I want to taste you."

I seal my lips around her clit once more, flicking it with my tongue even as I suckle at the swollen nub. My fingers are deep inside her, stretching her, stroking her, and she cries out as the orgasm crashes through her.

She's shaking, her thighs trembling, and the taste of her arousal is addictive. I lap at her folds, dragging every last drop of pleasure from her, and her moans are the sweetest music.

When she finally collapses back onto the rug, her body limp and sated, I crawl up over her, caging her in. Her eyes are hooded, her lips parted, and her hair is a halo around her. She's never looked more beautiful.

"Holly," I rasp, nuzzling her neck. "My Holly."

"Yes," she breathes. "Yours, Nick."

I slide a hand behind her back and unclasp her bra, tossing it aside. Her nipples are pink and puckered, and the sight makes my mouth water. I lean down and capture one in my mouth, and she lets out a sigh.

Her hands are on me, sliding down my front and wrapping around my cock just as her milk starts to flow into my mouth. The sweet, warm taste of her fills me, and the pleasure is exquisite. I moan against her breast, and she tightens her grip, stroking me slowly.

I can feel the tension coiling inside me, and I know I'm not going to last long. Not with her hands on me, her nipple in my mouth, her milk filling me up. It's too much, and not enough, and I need her more than I've ever needed anything.

I release her nipple and shift my hips, positioning the tip of my cock at her entrance. She's so wet, so ready for me, and it only takes the slightest pressure before her pussy yields to the thick crown of my cock.

"Oh, fuck," I groan, my jaw clenched.

Her eyes are wide, and she's breathing fast, her hands gripping my biceps.

"Nick," she gasps.

"I know, princess. Just relax."

I press forward, and her pussy stretches to accommodate my length. She's so tight, so fucking perfect, and the pleasure is almost painful. I grit my teeth, fighting the urge to thrust into her, and she whimpers.

"You're doing so good, princess. So good."

She's taking me inch by inch, her body quivering beneath mine, and when I'm finally fully seated inside her, we both let out a ragged sigh.

We stay like that for a moment, her pussy clenching around me, my cock pulsing inside her, and then I begin to move.

My thrusts are slow and deep, and she moans, her hips rising to meet mine. The sound is pure sin, and I can't believe how fucking perfect this is. How perfect she is.

My cock slides in and out of her, the slickness of her arousal making it easy for me to find the perfect rhythm. She's clinging to me, her nails digging into my back, and the slight sting of pain only heightens the pleasure.

I lean down and capture her mouth, our tongues tangling together. She's panting against my lips, her breath coming in soft gasps as I drive into her again and again.

"God, you feel so good," I groan, my hands cupping her breasts, my thumbs brushing her nipples. "So fucking good."

She arches her back, pushing her breast into my hand, and there's no way I can resist such a tempting invitation. So I dip my head and suck her nipple into my mouth, swallowing her milk even as I drive deeper into her.

The dual sensation seems to push her over the edge, and she cries out, her pussy clenching around me, her fingers tugging at my hair. Her orgasm spurs me on, and I thrust into her harder, faster, chasing my own release.

The pleasure is overwhelming, and I can feel my balls tightening as the pressure builds. I'm so fucking close, and the taste of her milk, the scent of her, the sound of her... it's all driving me wild.

"Are you ready for me to fill you, Holly? I'm gonna come so hard, gonna pump you full of my cum, and it's gonna take. It's gonna put a baby in you. Are you ready for that, princess?"

"Yes," she whimpers, her thighs clenching around my hips. "Oh God, yes."

"Say it," I growl, my thrusts getting rougher, more erratic. "Say you want me to come inside you."

"I want it," she moans, her pussy fluttering around my cock. "I want your cum, Nick. I want your baby growing inside me."

That's all it takes. The pressure breaks, and my orgasm slams through me. I roar her name, burying myself inside her, pumping her full of my seed. Her body is quivering beneath mine, her pussy milking me for every last drop.

We're both breathing hard, our bodies slick with sweat and tangled together, and it's the most incredible feeling. The closeness, the connection, the sheer ecstasy.

And the knowledge that I'm breeding her, that I'm filling her with my seed so her body can nurture it into a baby, just makes it feel even better.

I stroke a hand down her side, reveling in the feel of her skin, her warmth, her softness.

"Holly," I breathe.

"Yes, Nick?"

"You're mine now."

Her eyes widen, but there's no fear in them. No hesitation. Only understanding.

"I'm yours," she whispers.

"Good."

I brush a kiss across her forehead, her nose, her lips.

"Because I'm never letting you go."

And with that, I start kissing her again.

Kissing her, tasting her, and enjoying the best Christmas gift I've ever been given.

Epilogue

Holly

Christmas Morning - One Year Later:

There's crinkled red and green wrapping paper everywhere already, silver ribbons hanging off the edge of the coffee table, the soft crackle of the fireplace adding its warmth to the glow of the tree.

And then there's him.

Nick is crouched on the floor in front of the tree, pajama shirt rumpled, his hair mussed from sleep, and grinning like an absolute kid as he digs through the mountain of presents. He holds one up triumphantly, shaking it with mock suspense, then looks over his shoulder at me.

"One of these is the *good* one," he teases. "You'll never guess which."

I just laugh, shifting the sleepy weight of our son in my arms.

Luca. Our beautiful, perfect Luca. Just three months old and already so expressive. He's dozing now after his morning feed, soft puffs of breath against my chest, warm and heavy in his reindeer-print onesie. One little hand curls around the edge of my robe like he'll never let go.

"I don't need any more good ones," I murmur, brushing my lips over Luca's soft hair. "I've already got everything I ever wanted."

Nick glances at me again, and that heart-full, soul-full look he gives me every single day still melts me.

It's been a year since we met. Since he marched into my life in a Santa suit and gave me every fairytale ending I didn't know to wish for. Two months after that, he made me his wife. Since then, my whole world has been nothing but love and warmth and joy... and Nick. Always Nick.

And yes, he's spoiled me. Rotten. He says he can't help it and that I deserve everything. And he makes sure I have it.

He also makes sure the kids in our community do too. We spent yesterday hand-delivering packages to families in need again, just the same as last Christmas Eve. Only this time, Luca was strapped to my chest in a cozy little carrier while everyone cooed over him like he was the real star of the season.

Which, of course... he is.

Nick finally finds the box he was searching for. He brings it over and kneels beside the couch, placing it gently in my lap.

"It's nothing big," he says, even though there's a twinkle in his eye that tells me otherwise.

I arch a brow. "You say that every time. And then it turns out to be ridiculously over-the-top amazing."

He chuckles. "Open it and see."

I do. Slowly, carefully shifting Luca slightly to cradle him in one arm so I can tug the ribbon loose and lift the lid. Inside is a delicate diamond necklace. A single shimmering snowflake on a fine gold chain.

"Oh, Nick," I whisper, fingers brushing over the soft sparkle of it. "It's beautiful."

"So are you." He leans in and kisses my temple. "Merry Christmas, princess."

I blink back a tear. God, this man makes my heart ache in the best way.

"I have something for you too," I say softly.

He tilts his head, curious. "You do?"

I nod. My heart hammers, but not in a bad way. I lean close, lips brushing his ear as I whisper...

"I'm pregnant again."

He goes still for a second. Just a beat. Then he pulls back to look at me, eyes blazing with joy and disbelief all at once.

"Are you serious?"

I nod again, smiling so wide it hurts. "I took a test yesterday, but I wanted to wait until today to tell you."

Nick lets out a sound that's somewhere between a laugh and a growl, then cups my face in his hands and kisses me hard. Luca squirms slightly, letting out a soft squeak, and we both freeze.

"Sorry, little man," Nick murmurs, stroking his son's head gently. Then he grins at me again, eyes still shining. "You're giving me *another* gift this perfect? Holly... I love you so damn much."

"I love you too," I whisper.

Outside, snow has started to fall again, soft flakes catching on the window glass. Inside, everything glows. The fire, the tree, the warmth between us.

And in my arms, our son sighs contentedly, held between two people who will love him, and his sibling, with everything they have.

Christmas will never be the same again.

And I wouldn't have it any other way.

About the Author

Welcome to my wild, wicked world of *over-the-top, heart-pounding instalove*. I write fast-paced, **spicy age gap novellas** that don't waste time. They are just pure heat, obsession, and unapologetic desire from page one. If you're into dominant older heroes, eager younger heroines, and deliciously deviant themes like **breeding** and **lactation**, you're in the right place.

These days, all my stories revolve around one irresistible idea: **men who fall fast, fall hard, and never let go**. Think possessive, primal, borderline unhinged alphas who'd burn the world down for their girl. They're obsessed, they're intense, and yes, more than one has been lovingly described as a full-blown *caveman* by reviewers.

So whether you're here for the age gaps, the obsession, or the kind of heat that leaves scorch marks, you're in the right place. Get comfortable. It's about to get *feral*.

Find me online at https://allmylinks.com/willow-watkins

Printed in Dunstable, United Kingdom